THE BALLOON SAILORS

Text by
Diane Swanson

Illustrations by
Krystyna Lipka-Sztarballo

ANNICK PRESS

TORONTO + NEW YORK + VANCOUVER

"**Pop!**" goes the balloon that Woof catches with his teeth. Tamala and Abalon exchange worried looks, but it's not the burst balloon that upsets them. It's the fear they hear in their parents' low voices.

"Trouble is brewing," says Mother darkly, her fingers flying as she quilts.

Weary from working his shift at the mine, Father slumps down beside her. "King Zod is sick. He must give up the throne."

"But to the twins?" says Mother. "Prince Frack and Prince Frick **hate** each other. They always have. They always will."

"The king refuses to choose between them," Father sighs, burying his head in his hands. "He never has. He never will."

Two weeks pass, and the terrible news arrives.

"Hear ye!" cries a royal messenger. "King Zod has given the throne to his sons. Each one rules **half** the kingdom. Long live King Frack. Long live King Frick."

"Half the kingdom? What will that mean?" ask Tamala and Abalon, their voices trembling.

Mother wraps her arms tightly around them. "We don't know for sure but...all last night, the soldiers were working, building a wall of stone—thick and tall. It winds and it wanders, and it slices the kingdom exactly in two. Now no one can cross from this side to that, or from that side to this."

It's true! Just past the trees by the house stands the wall. The children—with Woof—check to see where it goes, but they scarcely can believe what they find.

Like a dam, the wall splits the pond where they fish. It chops old May's daisy bed almost in half. It carves up the schoolhouse—in two equal parts.

On and on winds the wall, making no sense at all. It cuts off the church from its very own graveyard. It holds back the cows from their trough and their barn. It keeps steam locomotives from reaching the station.

Back home again, Abalon cries, "What about Grandma and our cousin Peter? How are we ever to see them again?"

Mother's eyes fill with tears. Words lodge in her throat.

"We don't have an answer," Father shrugs sadly. "And I can't go to work if I can't cross the wall. Mother can't get to market to sell all her quilts."

The family falls silent. There's barely a breath.

Then Tamala speaks as she stares out the window. "At least, we'll send Grandma and Peter a note."

"We fear we **never** will see you again," she writes.

"Remember us… **always**," Abalon prints.

They tuck the short messages inside balloons, and they blow the balloons till they're both big and round.

Out in the yard, a strong wind is wailing. It lifts the balloons as the two children chant:

"Go, balloons, go! Rise and sail
Above the trees, on past the spire,
Across the pond to Peter's yard
Or Grandma's porch.
Go, balloons, go! Rise and sail."

"If only we could sail away, too," says Abalon wistfully.

"That's it!" cries Tamala. "We'll make ourselves a **gigantic** balloon."

Huddled and hushed inside the house, the family thinks of the things that they'll need: a **huge** pile of cloth to make a balloon and **plenty** of straw for a basket to ride in.

"There's something else," Father solemnly adds. "The balloon won't rise without hot air inside it. We need to have a gas burner too, but I just can't imagine wherever we'll find one."

The family knows there is so much to do, but they are determined to make their escape. "We'll search and we'll search till we get what we need," says Abalon firmly.

"But remember," warns Mother, "we must work in secret. King Frack and King Frick have their spies everywhere. Whoever's caught trying to sneak past the wall is punished and tossed into jail at once. Some people—it's said—have never, not ever, been seen again."

And so the children start gathering cloth — every bit, every scrap of cloth they can grab: the drapes from the windows, the sheets off the beds, Tamala's red satin skirt, Mother's polka-dot vest, Abalon's bright checkered shirt, and Father's long yellow scarf. They grab up Woof's bath rag — the one that's marked **"Woof."**

Day after day, they search for more cloth: old clothes from the neighbors, some rags from the shed, odd socks from the laundry, flour sacks from the mill.

Week after week, Mother is sewing. She's stitching each scrap of cloth to another. She's making the biggest balloon she can sew. It's as tall as the trees and as wide as the house.

Father is busily working as well. He's weaving a basket of straw to hold five—all of the family and Woof, too, of course. Then he ties the big basket to the jumbo balloon. Now all that he needs is a sturdy gas burner.

Night after night, the children hunt through the streets, looking
for something that just might do. At last, they head down to the dump
where they sift through the trash till they almost lose hope. Then
Abalon shouts, "Here's a gas burner! It's old and it's rusted, but still…
it might work." They cart it back home before the sun's up.

"You found one!" says Father, amazed. He tests the burner, but it sputters and spits. It flares up, then flickers, and finally, fizzles.

Nervously, Abalon and Tamala watch Father at work. He cleans out the burner, then tightens and oils it. He fiddles and fusses—till it burns bright and clear.

Now the family waits – waits for the wind to be blowing just right. Many nervous nights later, when it's ever so dark, they slip the huge balloon out of the house. Abalon watches for soldiers and spies as Father says quietly, "Let's climb aboard."

Frozen with fear, they try to be brave as flames from the burner heat up the cool air – and the cloth balloon billows and lifts as it fills.

The children chant softly, just under their breath:
"Go, balloon, go! Rise and sail
Above the trees, on past the spire,
Across the pond to Peter's yard
Or Grandma's porch.
Go, balloon, go! Rise and sail."

And it does! It **does**! The big balloon rises. It sails. It carries the family above the tall trees. It floats past the church spire—just missing the peak.

Then soldiers below fire their guns at the basket.

"Duck!" yells Mother, and the children crouch down. But the balloon keeps on sailing—right over the wall.

Abalon grins broadly and Tamala beams. Then they catch sight of Grandma. She's waving her arms. She's spotted the basket as it lands near her house.

"You made it!" she gasps. "You came after all!"

This story is just make-believe, but there really was a city split in two overnight. In 1961, East German soldiers built a wall between East and West Berlin. It cut through streets and gardens and parks. People in East Berlin couldn't go to their schools or jobs in West Berlin. They couldn't cross the wall to visit their families or friends.

In 1979, two East German families sewed a balloon that was four stories tall! They tied it to a big basket. One night, they climbed aboard and sailed over the wall.

After ten more years, the wall was knocked down. Berlin was one city again, and Germany, one country.

Words cannot express how much appreciation and respect I have for the people who turned their talents to this book: Krystyna Lipka-Sztarballo for her powerful and expressive paintings and Irvin Cheung for his clever and artistic design. A very special note of thanks goes to Dominica Babicki for smoothing the way. Her insight and patient efforts made this project possible. – D.S.

Annick Press Ltd.

We acknowledge the support of the Canada Council for the Arts, the Ontario Arts Council, the Government of Ontario through the Ontario Book Publishers Tax Credit program and the Ontario Book Initiative, and the Government of Canada through the Book Publishing Industry Development Program (BPIDP) for our publishing activities.

Copy edited by Elizabeth McLean
Design by Irvin Cheung / iCheung Design
The art in this book was rendered in watercolor with crayon and pencil.
The text was typeset in Corporate.

Cataloging in Publication
Swanson, Diane, 1944–
     The balloon sailors / written by Diane Swanson; illustrated by Krystyna Lipka-Sztarballo.

ISBN 1-55037-809-0

     1. Berlin Wall, Berlin, Germany, 1961–1989–Juvenile fiction. 2. Berlin (Germany)–History–1945–1990–Juvenile fiction. I. Lipka-Sztarballo, Krystyna II. Title.

PS8587.W3457B34 2003   jC813'.6   C2003-901494-0
PZ7

Manufactured in China

Published in the U.S.A. by
Annick Press (U.S.) Ltd.

Distributed in Canada by
Firefly Books Ltd.
3680 Victoria Park Avenue
Willowdale, ON
M2H 3K1

Distributed in the U.S.A. by
Firefly Books (U.S.) Inc.
P.O. Box 1338
Ellicott Station
Buffalo, NY 14205

Visit our website at: www.annickpress.com